ABOUT THE ENDPAPERS: The ancient domain of the Pawnee people was within the present states of Nebraska and northern Kansas. There are places which they greatly venerated—certain hills, rocky cliffs, springs of water, lakes, and caves. Tradition told that these sacred places were the doorways to the underground lodges of the *Nahurak,* the spirit birds and animals and all other living things waiting to be born. From season to season, *Tirawahat,* God, would cause the *Nahurak* to populate the land. It had always been that way.

In the drawing, multitudes of spirit horses, *Arusa,* surge up from the womb of Mother Earth, through the waters of a sacred lake, to spread out and replenish the wild herds. It was the wish of *Tirawaha*t that the *Nahurak* would give the Pawnee people a great many horses so they need never have to walk when they traveled in search of the buffalo herds. Kingfisher, *Rikutski,* leads the horses because he is the messenger who passes between our world and the lodge of the *Nahurak* beneath the water. It is nighttime, when such wonders happen, away from the eyes of people.

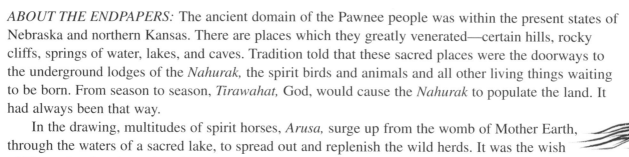

Mystic Horse

Mystic Horse
Copyright © 2003 by Paul Goble
Manufactured in China. All rights reserved.
www.harperchildrens.com

Library of Congress Cataloging-in-Publication Data
Goble, Paul.
Mystic horse / Paul Goble.
p.   cm.
Summary: After caring for an old abandoned horse, a poor young Pawnee boy is rewarded by the horse's mystic powers.
Includes bibliographical references.
ISBN 0-06-029813-8 — ISBN 0-06-029814-6 (lib. bdg.)
1. Pawnee Indians—Folklore.   2. Horses—Great Plains—Folklore.   [1. Pawnee Indians—Folklore.   2. Indians of North America—
Great Plains—Folklore.   3. Horses—Folklore.]   I. Title.
E99.P3 G63   2003   398.2'089'979—dc21   2002022831

1 2 3 4 5 6 7 8 9 10
❖
First Edition

The illustrations are drawn in pen and India ink, and painted with Winsor and Newton watercolor and gouache on Oram and Robinson
watercolor boards. Book design by Paul Goble.

The design, below, is Pawnee, early nineteenth century, depicting a sacred peace pipe
painted on a buffalo robe, which is now in the Field Museum of Natural History, Chicago.

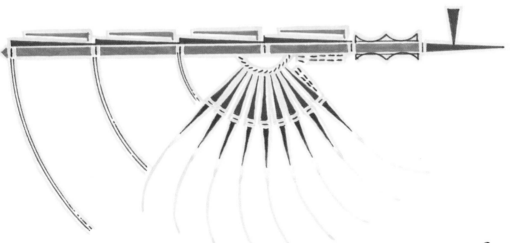

for Robert

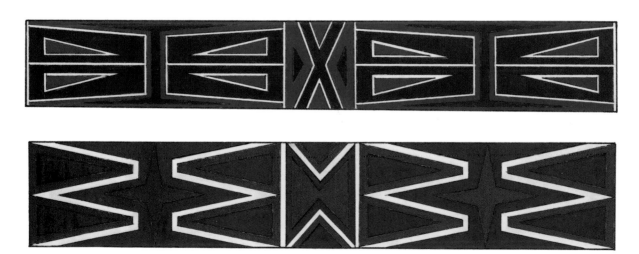

Mystic Horse

PAUL GOBLE

HarperCollins*Publishers*

REFERENCES: Cowdrey, Mike, *Arrow's Elk Society Ledger*, Morning Star Gallery, Santa Fe, 1999; Curtis, Natalie, *The Indians' Book*, Harper and Brothers, New York and London, 1907; Gilmore, Melvin R., *Prairie Smoke*, Columbia University Press, New York, 1929; Grinnell, George Bird, *Pawnee Hero Stories and Folk Tales*, Forest and Stream Publishing Company, New York, 1889; Grinnell, George Bird, *The Story of the Indian*, Chapman and Hall Ltd., London, 1896; Hyde, George E., *Pawnee Indians*, University of Denver Press, 1951; Weltfish, Gene, *The Lost Universe: Pawnee Life and Culture*, University of Nebraska Press, Lincoln, 1977.

Concerning horses: Curtin, Sharon, *Mustang*, Rufus Publications, Bearsville, NY, 1996; Ewers, John C., *The Horse in Blackfoot Indian Culture*, Smithsonian, Washington, DC, 1955; Ryden, Hope, *Mustangs: A Return to the Wild*, Viking Press, New York, 1972; Spragg, Mark, *Thunder of the Mustangs: Legend and Lore of the Wild Horses*, Sierra Club Books, San Francisco, 1997.

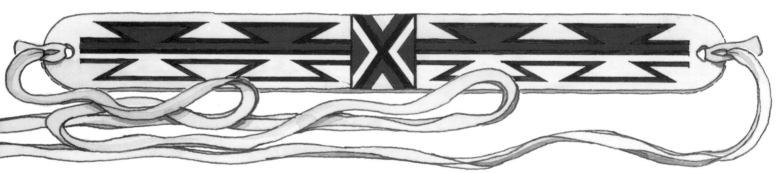

REFERENCES FOR THE DESIGNS: Pages 6 and 8, Pawnee buffalo hide burden straps (1850s), incised and painted designs. Straps were placed against the forehead or upper chest and the burden tied with hide thongs and carried on the back; Field Museum of Natural History, Chicago. Pages 10 and 31, Pawnee Morning Star designs carved in relief and painted on cradle boards; page 10, British Museum, London, England; page 31, from Nebraska State Historical Society photographs. Page 11, Pawnee drum (1902) with painted Thunderbird; Field Museum of Natural History, Chicago. Page 37, Pawnee buffalo hide shield (1820s), possibly depicting Sun and Moon, framed with Buffalo's protective horns and ears; British Museum, London, England.

ACKNOWLEDGMENTS: Mike Cowdrey, Fr. Peter Powell, Craig Howe, Kenny Harragarra, and Neil Gilbert: thank you for your knowlege and help; Ned Williams, Superintendent of Pawnee Public Schools, Pawnee, OK; Meccasue Simmons, Black Hills Wild Horse Sanctuary, Hot Springs, SD; Staci Veitch, American Humane Association, Englewood, CO; Jonathan King, British Museum, London, England; The Collections Department, Field Museum of Natural History, Chicago; and as always, thank you, my beloved wife, Janet.

This is based on an old Pawnee story, "The Dun Horse," published in *Pawnee Hero Stories and Folk Tales* by George Bird Grinnell in 1889. Prior to the Pawnees' move to Oklahoma, Grinnell spent several summers with them while they still lived in their traditional Nebraska homeland. He accompanied them on one of their last buffalo hunting expeditions, and perhaps it was sitting by the fire after eating roasted buffalo ribs that he listened to the old men tell the story of the Dun Horse. I have had to make changes from the original because certain aspects do not translate well into today's thinking, but I hope the spirit of the story is still there.

The Pawnee people seem to have been portrayed as warlike and brutal even as far back as the 1860s in R. M. Ballantyne's novel *Dog Crusoe*. In the recent movies *Little Big Man* and *Dances with Wolves*, they were pictured in an almost Nazi vein. History does not agree. They were civilized farmers living in earth-lodge villages, at peace with neighboring farming peoples. Perhaps the traditional plucked and shaped hairstyles, the multiple ear piercings, and pride in the naked and painted body have stirred some deep-seated fear in the white psyche, which has contributed to the bad press they have received over the years. . . .

This is a nineteenth-century story, at the time the white invasion had pressed tribe against tribe, and when the need for horses, which had been introduced by the Spanish, forced or tempted tribes to capture herds from one another. Horse raiding often resulted in battles between the tribes, and the Pawnees were justifiably fierce in defense of their horse herds and villages against the inexorable advance of the displaced Lakotas and Cheyennes. They never fought the U.S. military and were famous scouts in their pay during the last years of the Indian wars. Indeed, the Lakotas and Cheyennes, who were at war with the U.S. military, feared the Pawnee scouts far more than they did the soldiers.

Mention is made of touching, or striking, the enemy. This may seem puzzling, but in Plains warfare "counting coup" on an enemy, to strike or touch without killing, was demonstration of bravery. Acts of bravery could be retold many times later, a little like wearing medals. George Bird Grinnell wrote: "It was regarded as an evidence of bravery for a man to go into battle carrying no weapon that would do harm at a distance. It was more creditable to carry a lance than a bow and arrows; more creditable to carry a hatchet or a war-club than a lance; and the bravest thing of all was to go into a fight with nothing more than a whip, or a long twig—sometimes called a coup-stick."

This story, starting with the introductory song recorded in the early 1900s, tells us of the love Pawnee people had for their horses.

—Paul Goble, Rapid City, Black Hills, South Dakota

LONG AGO IN THE PAWNEE VILLAGE,
there was a man who dearly loved his horse,
but when the man died, his horse was no longer cared for,
and was continually passed from one person to another.
A friend of the man who had died dreamed that he saw
the dead man sitting with the drummers,
singing about his beloved horse.
When he awoke, he remembered the words, and the song
soon became popular among the Pawnee people:

Abandoned, lonely, unloved!
Abandoned, lonely, unloved!
Abandoned, lonely, unloved!
Our Father Above says:
There is an old horse in our midst
Who is without an owner,
Abandoned, lonely, unloved!

IN THOSE LONG AGO DAYS, when the Pawnee people had harvested their crops of corn and squash, they would leave their earth-lodge villages and travel out on the Great Plains to hunt buffalo. They had horses to ride and to carry their tipis and belongings when they went great distances in search of the wandering herds.

When they were not traveling, and the tipis were pitched, it was the responsibility of the older boys, the young men, to look after the herds of horses, and to guard the village. They would stay with the horses at pasture throughout the day, often far away from the camp. All the while they would keep a good lookout for enemies.

Traveling with the people were an old woman and her grandson. They were poor, living alone without any relatives at the edge of the village. Their only shelter was made of sticks and a patchwork of pieces of old tipi covers which people had thrown away. Nobody took much notice of them.

When the people moved from one camping place to another, the old woman and her grandson would stay behind to look for scraps of food, and to pick up discarded clothes. They had no horse. They walked, and what their dogs could not carry, they packed on their own backs. Their life was hard, but they were happy.

One day, as they followed far behind the village, they came upon a sad and sickly worn-out horse standing in the trail. He was terribly thin, with sores on his back.

"Grandmother," the boy said, "nobody wants this poor old horse. If we are kind and look after him, he will get well again. He will help us carry our packs! Then I will be able to join the buffalo hunt, and we will have meat, and fresh skins as well!"

And so they led the old horse, limping along behind them.
People laughed: "You've got yourself a great warhorse,
boy! How will we keep up with you now?"
But the boy loved his horse, and looked after him well.

After some days had passed, the boys who were out on the hills looking after the horses spotted enemies approaching on horseback. They quickly drove the herds back to the safety of the camp. The men grabbed their weapons, mounted their fastest horses, and rode out to meet the enemy.

The boy, riding the poor old horse, followed shyly at a distance. But the men pointed at the horse and laughed: "Look! Here's the one who'll leave us all behind! Boy, that's an old good-for-nothing half-starved horse. You'll be killed. Go back home!"

The boy was ashamed, and rode off to one side where he could not hear their unkind remarks. The horse turned his head and spoke to the boy: "Listen to me! Take me down to the river and cover me with mud." The boy was alarmed to hear him speak, but without hesitation he rode to the river and daubed mud all over his horse.

Then the horse spoke again: "Don't take your bow and arrows. Cut a long willow stick instead. Then ride me, as hard as you can, right into the enemy's midst and strike their leader with the stick, and ride back again. Do it four times, and the enemy will be afraid; but do not do it more than four times!"

While the horse was speaking, he was tossing his head, stamping and prancing this way and that, until the boy could hardly hold him back. He loosened the reins, and the horse galloped toward the enemy. He was no longer an old sickly worn-out horse! He flew like a hawk, right to where the enemy riders were formed up in line of battle. The boy struck their leader with his willow stick, turned, and rode back to his people with arrows flying past him like angry wasps.

He turned again without stopping, and the horse carried him back to strike another enemy rider. By then his people were cheering loudly. Four times the boy charged back and forth, and each time he hit one of the enemy, just as his horse had told him.

The men watched the boy with amazement. Now they, too, felt brave enough to follow his example, and they drove the enemy in full retreat from the village. It was like chasing buffalo.

The boy was eager to join the chase. He said to himself: "I have struck four times, and I have not been hurt. I will do it once more." And so, again, he rode after the retreating enemy riders. He whipped another with his stick, but at that very instant his horse was pierced by an arrow, and fell. The horse tried to stand, but he could not.

When the enemy had fled, the men returned and gathered round the boy. His horse was dead. They wanted to touch the horse, for they knew he had been no ordinary one, but a horse with mystic powers.

The leader spoke: "Today this boy has shown that he is braver than all of us. From now on we will call him Piraski Resaru, Boy Chief."

But the boy cried. He was sad for his horse, and angry with himself that he had not done what the mysterious horse had told him. He untied the lariat, pulled out the arrow, and carefully wiped away the blood.

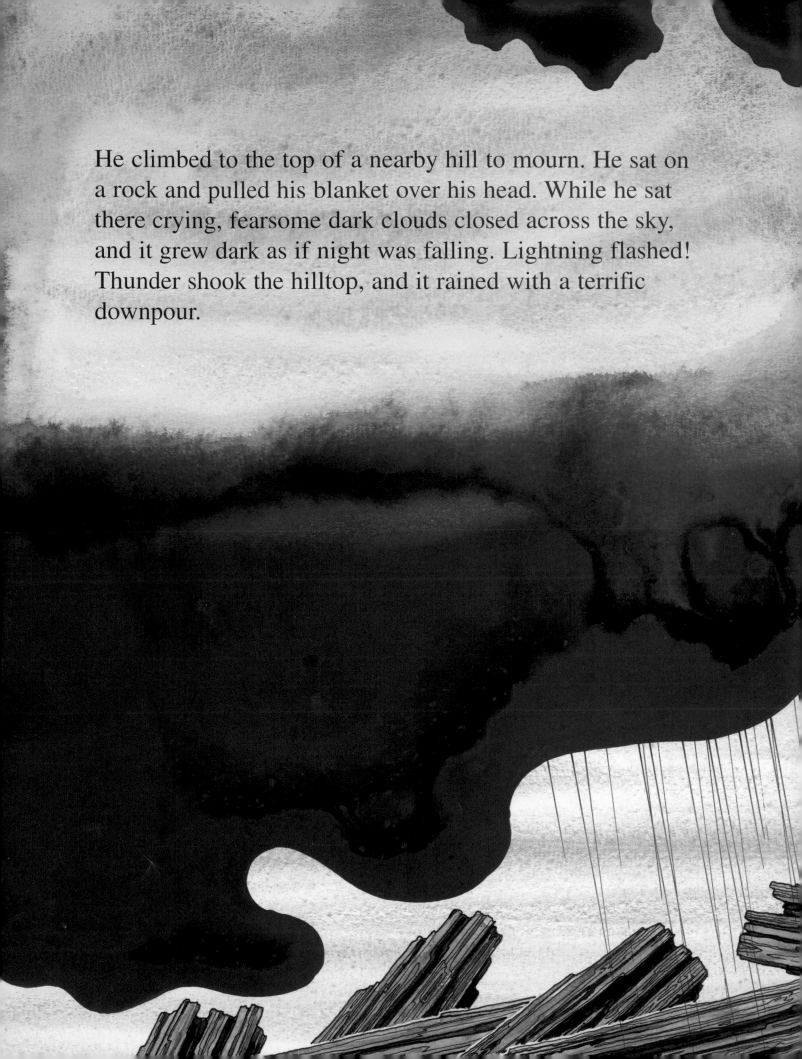

He climbed to the top of a nearby hill to mourn. He sat on a rock and pulled his blanket over his head. While he sat there crying, fearsome dark clouds closed across the sky, and it grew dark as if night was falling. Lightning flashed! Thunder shook the hilltop, and it rained with a terrific downpour.

Looking through the downpour, he imagined he saw the dead horse move his legs a little, and that he even tried to lift his head. He wondered if something strange and wonderful was happening. And then he knew it was true: the horse slowly stretched out his front legs, and then stood up!

The boy was a little afraid, but he ran down from the hilltop and clasped his arms round the horse's neck, crying with joy that he was alive again.

The horse spoke softly to him: "Tirawahat, Our Father Above, is good! He has forgiven you. He has let me come back to you."

The storm passed; the rain stopped. All was still and fresh, and the sun shone brilliantly on his beautiful living horse. "Now take me up into the hills, far away from people," the horse told him. "Leave me there for four days, and then come for me."

When the four days had passed, Boy Chief left the village
and climbed into the pine tree hills.

A horse neighed, and the mysterious horse appeared,
followed by a herd of spirited horses. They surrounded
Boy Chief, snorting and stamping excitedly, horses of
every color—beautiful bays, chestnuts, shiny blacks,
whites, grays, and paints.

Mounted on his mysterious horse, Boy Chief drove the horses round and round the village. He stopped in front of his grandmother's shelter.

"Grandmother," he said, "now you will always have horses! You need never walk again! Choose the ones you want, and give the rest to those who need them most." And so it was done.

After that, the boy and his grandmother rode whenever they moved camp. They lived in a tipi and were not poor any longer. And, just as his grandmother had looked after him when he was young, so he, too, always took good care of her for all her years.

LEGEND TELLS
that Piraski Resaru, Boy Chief,
never made the wonderful horse work,
but that he loved to ride him on special occasions.
He would paint lightning streaks down the horse's legs,
because he could run faster than any horse,
and he would tie eagle feathers in his mane and tail,
for the honors won defending the village.
Then horse and rider would share the wonder and the
beauty around them, the ground beneath, and the sky above.
"Ah yes!" people would say.
"It's good to see Boy Chief and his mystic horse!"

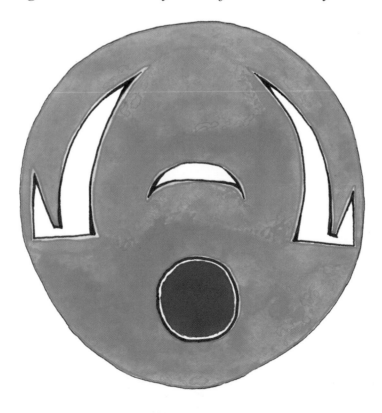